SADDLEBACK *Classics*

The Hunchback of Notre Dame

VICTOR HUGO

ADAPTED BY

Emily Hutchinson

SADDLEBACK
EDUCATIONAL PUBLISHING

ISE #7

SADDLEBACK *Classics*

The Adventures
of Huckleberry Finn

The Adventures
of Tom Sawyer

The Call of the Wild

A Christmas Carol

The Count of Monte Cristo

Dr. Jekyll and Mr. Hyde

Dracula

Frankenstein

Great Expectations

Gulliver's Travels

The Hound of
the Baskervilles

**The Hunchback
of Notre Dame**

Jane Eyre

The Jungle Book

The Last of the Mohicans

The Man in the Iron Mask

Moby Dick

Oliver Twist

Pride and Prejudice

The Prince and
the Pauper

The Red Badge
of Courage

Robinson Crusoe

The Scarlet Letter

Swiss Family Robinson

A Tale of Two Cities

The Three Musketeers

The Time Machine

Treasure Island

The War of the Worlds

White Fang

Development and Production: Laurel Associates, Inc.
Cover and Interior Art: Black Eagle Productions

SADDLEBACK
EDUCATIONAL PUBLISHING

Three Watson
Irvine, CA 92618-2767

Website: www.sdlback.com

ISBN-10: 1-56254-525-6
ISBN-13: 978-1-56254-525-3
eBook: 978-1-60291-362-2

Printed in the United States of America
12 11 10 09 08 07   9 8 7 6 5 4 3 2

CONTENTS

1 Quasimodo

The good people of Paris were awakened by a grand peal from all the bells in the city. January 6, 1482, was a double holiday. It was the Feast of the Epiphany and the Feast of Fools. Today there would be fireworks, a tree-planting, and a play.

All the houses and shops were closed that morning. Crowds of people made their way toward the fireworks or the play. Hardly anyone went to the tree-planting.

The Palace of Justice was already quite crowded. No one wanted to miss the election of the Pope of Fools. This event would take place after the play.

It was not easy to get into the great hall of the palace. Thousands of people filled the area. Their ears were stunned by the noise. Their eyes were dazzled by the beauty of the palace. They were amazed by the towering arches, carved wood, and gold trim. The floor was made of the finest black and white marble. Pictures of all the kings of France adorned the walls. The tall, pointed windows were made of lovely stained glass.

The rich marble table was very long, broad, and thick. On it was a very tall wooden cage. The upper floor of the cage was easy to see from every part of the hall. This would be the stage for the play. The lower part of the cage was covered by fabric to hide the actors' dressing room. A ladder was used for stage entrances and exits.

When the clock struck 12, it was time for the play to start.

The crowd fell silent. Every eye was fixed on the marble table. Nothing could be seen but the four sergeants who were guarding the stage. These men stood as stiff and still as four painted statues.

The crowd waited 15 minutes. Nothing happened. No one appeared on the platform or the stage. The crowd grew restless.

Finally, one man said, "Let us have the

play—or I say we should hang the sergeants!"

The four sergeants turned pale and looked at each other. The angry crowd started to move toward them.

Just then, the dressing room curtains opened. A young man, shaking with fear, came out and began to bow.

"Ladies and gentlemen," the young man announced nervously, "tonight we have the honor of performing before the Cardinal. He's not here right now. We shall begin when he arrives."

The mob began hooting. "We want to see the play! Begin immediately!"

The man who had come out to make the announcement trembled. He didn't know what to do. He was afraid of being hanged—hanged by the people for making them wait, or hanged by the Cardinal for not waiting. Either way, he would lose!

Luckily for him, another person came forward. It was a tall, slender young man with sparkling eyes and smiling lips. His name was Pierre Gringoire. He was the author of the play. "Begin the play right now," he ordered.

"I will explain to the Cardinal."

And so the play began. The audience had trouble following it. The only person who seemed to be enjoying the play was its author! The audience was distracted by a beggar who had climbed up a pillar near the stage. Soon he distracted even the actors on the stage. They stopped performing.

"Why do you stop? Go on! *Go on!*" yelled Gringoire. No sooner had the actors obeyed him than there was another distraction. The door of the reserved platform opened. The usher announced: "The Cardinal."

Poor Gringoire! Nobody paid attention to his play. All heads were turned toward the platform. His play was cut short a second time! Everyone in the audience tried to get a look at the Cardinal, followed by his staff of abbots and bishops. He bowed and smiled before sitting on his red velvet chair. The people in the audience watched intently, pointing out the churchmen they recognized and telling their names.

The Duke of Austria, along with his 48 ambassadors, entered soon after. Again, the audience stared as they were seated. Each dignitary was announced by the usher. There were a thousand whispers at each name. Meanwhile, the four actors on the stage were completely forgotten by the audience. This is just what poor Pierre Gringoire had feared!

At first, Gringoire asked the actors to raise their voices and go on. Then, seeing that nobody was listening, he ordered them to stop. For a quarter of an hour, the performers patiently stood on stage, waiting for the audience to quiet down.

At last the play began again, but the audience had lost interest. One man shouted, "People of Paris! This play is not amusing. Nothing happens! I thought we were going to select the Pope of Fools. In my city of Ghent, this is how we do it: A crowd such as this one gathers. Then anyone who chooses puts his head through a hole and makes an ugly face. The one who makes the ugliest face is chosen Pope. That's it! It's a lot of fun, I tell you. Shall we choose your Pope of Fools this way? It will surely be more amusing than watching any more of this boring play."

The audience clapped in agreement. Someone broke the glass out of a small round window. Then people started putting their heads through the empty circle of stone. Every human expression was seen. Men and women, young and old, scholars and shopkeepers—all got in on the fun. At last the Pope of Fools was elected. "Hurrah, hurrah, hurrah!" the people called out on all sides.

A truly ugly face had peered out of the hole. The nose was big and oddly formed. The mouth was shaped like a horseshoe. A coarse eyebrow arched over the small left eye. The right eye was completely buried under an enormous growth. The teeth were jagged. One tooth stuck out like an elephant's tusk. The chin was forked. Above all, the look on this unfortunate face showed a mix of spite, wonder, and sadness.

The new Pope of Fools was brought out in triumph. It was then that everyone realized the man had not been making a face—this was his *real* face! Indeed, his whole body was ugly. His head was covered with coarse red hair. Between his shoulders rose an enormous hump. His legs were strangely put together, and his hands and feet were huge. Still, there was an air of strength and courage about him. He looked like a giant who had been broken into pieces and then carelessly reassembled.

People in the crowd began to shout. "It is the bell-ringer, Quasimodo! Oh, yes, it is Quasimodo, the hunchback of Notre Dame! Quasimodo, the one-eyed! Quasimodo, the bowlegged! Hurrah! Hurrah!" A woman spoke to him, but he did not answer. "He is deaf," a man near her explained. "He became deaf from ringing the bells."

Quasimodo was crowned with the fake tiara and the mock robe of the Pope of Fools. Then he was made to sit down on a special chair. Twelve men carried the chair upon their shoulders. Quasimodo looked down on the handsome, well-shaped men who were carrying him. A strange kind of joy seemed to spread over his sad face. Then the parade proceeded through the palace and out into the streets.

2   **Esmeralda**

Night comes early in January. It was already dark when Gringoire left the Palace. He could not return to his apartment, for he was six months behind in his rent. He had hoped to be paid for his play—but that didn't happen. Where would he go to find lodging for the night? The answer was easy. He could choose any pavement in Paris!

While crossing the Palace square, poor Gringoire saw the Pope of Fools coming. The band that had played at his play was now playing for the parade. Another reminder of his play's failure!

Shivering in the cold, he wandered through the city, looking for a place to sleep. When he saw a big bonfire in one of the city squares, Gringoire headed toward it. Perhaps someone would give him some food. A group of people was there, trying to stay warm.

A young female was dancing in an open space between the crowd and the fire. At first, Gringoire could not decide whether she was a human being, a fairy, or an angel. The golden-skinned girl was slender, elegant, and graceful. Gringoire watched as she played a tambourine and danced on an old Persian carpet spread on the ground. Her beautiful black eyes flashed like lightning.

Every eye was fixed upon her, every mouth open. She seemed like a supernatural creature. Just then, one of her curls got loose, and a small brass object fell from it. She bent down to pick it up. At that moment, Gringoire realized that the lovely creature was indeed human. "Aha!" he thought. "A gypsy!"

One man watched the dance with intense interest. Nearly hidden by the surrounding crowd, he was bald except for a few tufts of thin, gray hair at his temples. His brow was already wrinkled. But his eyes showed an expression of youth, life, and passion. As he watched the girl dance, this man seemed to become more and more gloomy!

When the girl stopped dancing, the crowd around her cheered and clapped.

"Djali!" the gypsy girl cried.

A pretty little white goat trotted up to her. Its hooves and horns were painted gold, and it wore a gold necklace. The goat had been crouching on a corner of the carpet, watching her mistress dance.

"Djali," said the dancer. "Now it's your turn." She sat down beside the goat and held up her tambourine. "Djali," she said, "what month of the year is it?" The goat lifted her front foot and hit the tambourine once. It was in fact the first month. The crowd applauded.

"Djali," said the girl, "what day of the month is it?" Djali hit the tambourine six times. "Djali," said the gypsy, "what time is it?" The goat struck seven times. At just that moment, the tower clock struck seven. The astonished crowd cheered even louder. "Hurrah for Esmeralda and Djali!" they cried.

"She must be a witch!" a voice called out. It was the bald man in the black cloak.

The girl trembled and turned away, but the applause began again. Smiling, the girl began to pass her tambourine around.

Silver and copper coins, large and small, clattered into the tambourine. Gringoire was embarrassed when she came to him. He had not a penny to give her.

Just then, the parade of the Pope of Fools passed by. Quasimodo bowed and waved to the crowds. For the first time in his life, he felt very important. He didn't realize that the crowd was mocking him, so he smiled sweetly through his broken teeth.

Then the gloomy man in the black cloak dashed from the big crowd. He snatched Quasimodo's fake tiara from his head. "You are making a fool of yourself!" he yelled.

Seeing that it was the Archdeacon Claude Frollo, Quasimodo gasped. He dropped to his knees before the man. As the bell-ringer of Notre Dame, Quasimodo worked for him.

Frollo made Quasimodo follow him down a dark alley. No one tried to stop them. Everyone was afraid of Quasimodo's strength.

*　*　*　*

Gringoire's stomach started to growl. "I *must* find some supper soon! But where?"

He took it into his head to follow Esmeralda. "Why not?" he thought. "I have nowhere else to go. And who knows? The gypsies are said to be very good-natured. Maybe they'll feed me."

Gringoire followed Esmeralda and Djali deeper and deeper into the maze of dark streets. Esmeralda looked over her shoulder a few times, suspicious that she was being followed. Suddenly, Gringoire heard her scream! He turned the shadowy corner and saw her struggling with two men.

Gringoire advanced boldly. "Stop!" he cried. Then he noticed that one of the men was Quasimodo and the other one was the Archdeacon Frollo. The hunchback struck Gringoire and sent him reeling. Then Quasimodo ran back and picked up the young girl. He carried her gently—as if she were a silken scarf. The other man followed, and the goat ran after all three.

"Murder! *Murder!*" Esmeralda cried out.

Some passing horsemen from the king's bodyguard heard her call. They jumped down from their horses and snatched her from

Quasimodo. Seeing this, the archdeacon disappeared into the shadows.

Quasimodo was quickly surrounded and tied up. He roared and foamed at the mouth. He furiously kicked and bit.

Esmeralda gracefully leapt up onto the officer's saddle. "You saved me! What is your name, sir?" she asked.

"My name is Captain Phoebus. I am at your service, dear lady."

"Thank you," she said. Then she slid down from his horse and vanished like lightning.

Still stunned by the hunchback's blow, Gringoire watched as the soldiers dragged Quasimodo away. Then he realized again how very cold and hungry he was.

He walked on alone toward the saddest corner of the city. Fires blazing here and there lit the walls of crumbling houses. Homeless people huddled together to keep warm. The poor swarmed around Gringoire like flies.

"*Money!*" they cried out.

"But I have nothing!" Gringoire explained. "I am only a poet."

The beggars refused to take no for an

answer. Finally, one of them said, "Let's take him to King Clopin!"

Three of the beggars grabbed Gringoire and dragged him away. They went into the Court of Miracles tavern—the home of Paris's thieves, beggars, and outcasts. A great fire burned upon a large, round hearth. Tables were placed here and there at random. Near the fire, sitting on a broken barrel, was the same beggar who had disrupted the play that afternoon!

The beggar was in fact Clopin, King of the Outcasts. He watched as Gringoire was hauled before him. "Who have we here?" he asked in a booming voice.

"I am a poet!" Gringoire stammered. "My play was performed today in the great hall of the palace."

Clopin sneered. "Oh, really? Well, I was there, too. All the more reason to hang you! That play was very annoying."

Gringoire shuddered. Clopin thought for a moment. He whispered to some of the other outcasts. Then he said, "We won't hang you if you become one of us. Prove yourself as a pickpocket, and we will let you live."

Clopin pointed to a kind of scarecrow hanging above a three-legged stool. The figure wore a red suit covered with small bells. "Stand on that stool," Clopin commanded. "Take the wallet from the scarecrow's pocket. If the bells don't clatter, you can go."

Gringoire was nervous. "But what if a gust of wind comes along?" he asked.

"That's easy—you'll be hanged!"

Gringoire climbed up on the stool and reached out his arm. But just as he touched the scarecrow, he lost his balance. The sounds of a hundred bells filled the air.

"*Hang him!*" Clopin cried out.

But then he smiled and stood up. "Wait! I forgot about our custom! We never hang a man until the women have been given a chance to marry him. This way, ladies! A husband for free! Who wants him?"

An old hag, terribly ugly, eagerly stepped forward. "Do you have any money in your purse?" she asked Gringoire in a raspy voice.

Gringoire looked down at her. "No—not a single cent," he answered truthfully.

The old hag scowled. "Hang, then, and welcome to it!" she said in disgust.

"Anyone else?" Clopin cried. "I'll count to three. One, two . . ."

"I'll take him!" It was Esmeralda. She had come from the back of the room.

Now Gringoire was sure he had been in a dream since that morning.

"Drat!" Clopin snorted. "I was *so* looking forward to a good hanging!"

Someone handed Gringoire a clay jug. "Now throw it to the ground," Esmeralda said. The pitcher broke into four large pieces.

"You must stay married to him for four years!" Clopin declared.

"Very well," Esmeralda replied. "But I've only married him to save him from being hanged." With that, she took Gringoire by the hand and led him to her room.

§3 | Claude Frollo

Some 16 years before Esmeralda married Gringoire, a child had been left at Notre Dame Cathedral. To the left of the great church's front door was a wooden bed sealed in the pavement. It was the custom to put orphans here. Anyone who chose to could take them away. A copper basin for donations was placed in front of the bed.

It was Quasimodo Sunday, one week after Easter. The child who had been left that day was being inspected by two old women.

"How strange! What can it be?"

"It can't really be a *child*, Agnes. Maybe it's a deformed ape."

"It's so ugly! Perhaps we should throw it into the river or the fire."

"Surely no one will claim this one! I don't think it's really a baby. My guess is that this little monster is about four years old."

Indeed, it was not a newborn baby. It was a twitching mass of humanity in a canvas bag. The head peeping out was very disfigured! There was a forest of red hair, one eye, a mouth, and a few teeth. The eye was weeping, the mouth was crying, and the teeth seemed to want only to bite.

A young priest had been listening to the women talking. He pushed by the women, looked at the child, and stretched out his hand. "I'll adopt this child," he said.

He picked up the screaming bundle and carried it away. The young priest was none other than Claude Frollo. He named the child after the day—*Quasimodo*.

Frollo himself had a very interesting history. From childhood, his parents had trained him for the priesthood. While still very young, he had been sent away to study. He learned to read Latin, Greek, and Hebrew. By age 18, he believed that life had but one purpose—to learn.

But that all changed in 1466. Paris was very hot that summer. More than 40,000 people died of a plague. Among those who died were Claude Frollo's parents. A little brother, a baby, was left behind. Claude was the last remaining adult in the Frollo family. He took the baby under his care. Before, he had thought only of books. Now he began to live!

Claude Frollo's feelings for his brother transformed him. At last he discovered the joy of love! At that time, though, he believed that the love of family was all a person needed. He thought that loving a little brother would be enough to fill his life.

Claude threw himself into caring for little Jehan. He was more than a brother to the baby—he was the child's mother and father!

He had been taking care of Jehan for about a year when he heard the old women talking about the deformed orphan. When he looked at the unlucky creature, he was moved by deep compassion. He vowed in his heart to rear the child for the love of his brother. What if Jehan might prove to have some faults in the future? Perhaps this charity done in his name might be placed to his credit.

*   *   *   *

The night Esmeralda married Gringoire, Quasimodo had been the bell-ringer at Notre Dame for several years. This was thanks to his foster father, Claude Frollo. Quasimodo loved his job. He felt as one with the great church of Notre Dame. He'd grown up inside it. He was familiar with every inch of its walls, floors, and ceilings. The church had been his nest, his home, his country—his universe!

But an evil fate seemed to stalk the poor orphan. The sound made by the huge bells had broken Quasimodo's eardrums. He became deaf at 14. Before this, his hearing was the only thing that was normal about him. Now his soul was plunged into profound darkness. His sadness had become as complete as his ugliness! From the moment he lost his hearing, he decided to keep silent. In a way, this protected him from other people's mocking laughter.

His favorite activity was ringing the bells. When he pulled the ropes, the whole tower trembled. It was the only sound that broke through the silence.

Quasimodo hated all human beings except one. He loved Claude Frollo as much as—perhaps more than—his cathedral. This was easy to understand. The young priest had accepted him, adopted him, and taken care of him. Claude Frollo had made him the bell-ringer of Notre Dame! Quasimodo would have done anything to please his only friend. At Frollo's signal, he would even have jumped from the top of the great towers!

In 1482, Quasimodo was about 20 years old. Claude Frollo had turned 36. The priest was still involved in the education of his younger brother, Jehan. But this project had caused him bitterness. Jehan had grown up to be wild, lazy, and ignorant. He was more interested in having fun than in studying.

This saddened his older brother. He threw himself even more into the study of science. As a priest, he became more learned and more severe. As a man, he became sour and gloomy. People began to talk. They wondered why Frollo's head was always bowed. They asked why he sighed so often. Rightly or wrongly, the people of Paris had become afraid of him.

Claude Frollo had always stayed away from women. But now he seemed to *hate* them— especially gypsy women. He had asked the bishop to forbid gypsies from dancing in the square. He was outraged when the bishop refused. For some reason he seemed to be out for revenge. He began to collect information about all the wizards and witches who'd been burned or hanged in the past.

4 Paquette

On the day following the Feast of Fools, Quasimodo was put on trial. The courtroom was packed. Everyone knew that the Pope of Fools had tried to steal a gypsy dancer. The trial judge entered the courtroom and made his way to the big oak chair. "Silence in the court!" he ordered loudly.

Quasimodo was brought in, tied up and heavily guarded. The judge read out the charges against him.

"Your name?" the judge asked.

Because he had not heard the question, Quasimodo looked at the judge without answering. The judge was quite deaf himself. Not knowing about Quasimodo's deafness, he thought the hunchback had answered. "Very well," he said. "Your age?"

Quasimodo remained silent. But again,

the judge assumed that his question had been answered. "Your job?" he asked.

Still Quasimodo was silent. The people in the courtroom began to whisper and glance around at one another.

Thinking Quasimodo had answered, the judge continued. "You are charged with disturbing the peace and trying to kidnap a young girl. How do you plead—guilty or not guilty?" Still, Quasimodo said nothing.

"Clerk, have you recorded the prisoner's answers so far?" the judge asked.

At this question, a roar of laughter burst from the audience. The judge supposed they were laughing at something Quasimodo had said. So he went on, frowning at the crowd's rudeness.

But the judge had lost his temper. "Is the prisoner daring to make fun of me?" he demanded. "For your disrespect, you will be whipped for an hour! Take him away!"

The clerk felt sorry for the poor victim. He whispered into the judge's ear, "But your honor—the poor fellow is deaf."

The judge, however, didn't hear the

clerk—although he pretended to. "Aha!" he said. "That is a different thing. I did not know that. In this case, let the prisoner have *another* hour in the pillory!"

* * * *

Outside the courthouse, three women and a small boy were walking down the street. The boy looked longingly at a small cake he was carrying in one chubby hand. His mother, Mahiette, was dragging him along.

The cake was for Sister Gudule, a poor recluse who could not take care of herself. Some great sorrow had caused her hair to turn gray when she was quite young. No one in Paris knew anything about her past—except that she hated gypsies. Whenever she saw one, she would yell out threats and curses. The good women of Paris kept her alive by taking her gifts of food and water.

The three women were talking all at once. "Hurry!" said the first. "Let's not be late. They are going to whip the bell-ringer at the pillory. I don't want to miss it."

"Look there!" said the second. "A crowd is gathered by the bridge. What's going on?"

"Listen! I hear a tambourine," said the first woman. "It must be young Esmeralda playing tricks with her goat."

"The gypsy!" Mahiette cried, grabbing the little boy's arm. "Let's get out of here! She might steal my son!"

"Where did you get such an idea?" the first woman asked.

"She's not the only one who fears the gypsies," the second woman said. "Sister Gudule has the same opinion. No one knows why she feels that way. But why do you?"

"Oh," said Mahiette, "I will tell you why. In the village where I was born, I grew up with a young woman named Paquette. When she was 18—this would be 16 years ago—she had a beautiful child, a girl with dark curly hair. Paquette loved that baby with a joy that cannot be described. She sewed beautiful dresses for her and made her a pair of pink shoes no bigger than a thumb. Every day she thanked God for the gift of this child.

"When the baby was a year old, a group of gypsies came to the area. They camped on a hill outside town. They studied people's palms and predicted future events. Poor Paquette was curious. She wanted to know about her daughter's future, so she carried the baby to the gypsy camp. The gypsies admired the infant, hugging and kissing her. Above all, they praised her tiny feet and her pretty little shoes. The fortune teller said the baby would have good luck. Paquette was overjoyed. The baby was to be a good and beautiful *queen*!

"The next day, Paquette slipped out for a moment while the infant lay sleeping. Leaving the door ajar, she went to tell a friend what the gypsies had said about her baby. When she returned, she didn't hear the baby crying. 'That's lucky!' she said to herself. 'The baby is still asleep.' But then she found that the infant was gone! Nothing was left except one of its pretty little shoes. In her place was a strange little monster. It was an ugly, one-eyed, limping thing—about four years old.

"Later, the people of the village went to the gypsies' camp. There they found the remains of a large fire, bits of ribbons that had been on the baby's dress, and some drops of blood. They had no doubt that the gypsies had killed the baby in one of their strange rituals. Poor Paquette! The next day her hair had turned completely gray. The day after that, she disappeared."

"And what happened to the monster left by the gypsies?" asked the first woman.

"Oh, that child was sent to Paris. He was left at Notre Dame as an orphan."

Mahiette was new to Paris. She didn't realize that the baby and Quasimodo were one and the same.

Still talking, the women came to the place where Quasimodo was to be punished. A large crowd had already gathered at the pillory. It was a terrible sight. Everyone could see the agony on Quasimodo's face as he was being whipped. After the whipping, the hunchback was displayed in public view for another hour.

The women hurried on to visit Sister Gudule. When they arrived, Mahiette could not believe what she saw. The withered figure seemed to be in a trance. She was staring at something in her hand—a tiny pink shoe. It was the very shoe the gypsies had left behind when they stole Paquette's baby!

"Aha! This woman may be *called* Sister Gudule," Mahiette explained to her friends. "But her real name is Paquette." At this, the three women began to weep.

Meanwhile, at the pillory, Quasimodo had raised his head to look out at the crowd. "Water!" he cried out pitifully. But nobody gave him any. "Water!" he cried again. Then, at last, one woman came forward carrying a cup of water. It was the gypsy, Esmeralda! As it happened, Sister Gudule—or Paquette—looked out her window at just that moment.

"Curses on you, gypsy! Be cursed, you stealer of children! *Cursed! Cursed!*"

5 Phoebus

Several weeks went by. It was a mild spring day in early March. Near Notre Dame, a group of wealthy young ladies stood on the balcony of a fine house. Captain Phoebus was there with a young woman named Fleur-de-Lys. She and the captain were engaged to be married. Phoebus, however, had secretly become very bored with Fleur-de-Lys. He preferred to be laughing with his friends in the tavern and flirting with the women there. Today, it was all he could do to be polite to Fleur-de-Lys and her friends. He was sorry they were engaged. The idea of marrying no longer appealed to him. But he had no idea how to get out of it.

Just then, Fleur-de-Lys saw a young gypsy girl dancing in the square below. She had a little white goat with her. Fleur-de-Lys turned to Phoebus and said, "Did you not tell us that you saved a young gypsy woman from being kidnapped?"

"Yes, I did," Phoebus said.

"Look," said Fleur-de-Lys, pointing to the square. "Is that your gypsy girl?"

Phoebus glanced at the gypsy and nodded.

"Well, since you know her, why don't you ask her to come up? It would be amusing if she danced for us."

"Why not?" Phoebus said. He called down to Esmeralda.

When Esmeralda saw him, she stood still. Then she smiled and blushed deeply. After a moment's thought, she picked up her tambourine and made her way across the street. Soon, Esmeralda and Djali, her goat, were inside the fine house.

"Do you remember me, pretty girl?" Phoebus asked Esmeralda.

"Oh, yes!" Esmeralda said softly.

"Come now!" Fleur-de-Lys scolded. It was clear that she envied Esmeralda's beauty. She was worried that Phoebus would pay too much attention to the pretty girl. "We do not pay you to *talk*, girl! Dance for us!"

"Not just yet," Phoebus said. "First, please tell us your name."

"Esmeralda."

Fleur-de-Lys was burning with jealousy. She clapped her hands for Esmeralda to start dancing. Instead, Esmeralda emptied a pouch that hung around Djali's neck. Some little blocks with letters on them fell to the carpet. Djali played with the blocks, arranging them to spell the word *Phoebus*.

Fleur-de-Lys gasped when she saw what Djali had done. "I knew it!" she said. "The goat is under a spell! The girl is a witch!"

Esmeralda was frightened. After quickly picking up the little blocks, she ran down the stairs with Djali.

Phoebus smiled. He was flattered that the gypsy had taught the goat to spell his name. He put on his cloak and followed Esmeralda down to the street.

Earlier, Claude Frollo had been watching from the north tower of Notre Dame. He had seen Esmeralda dancing in the square. Now, when he saw her running out of Fleur-de-Lys's house, he dashed down the spiral staircase. As he passed the bell tower, he noticed that Quasimodo had also been staring down at the beautiful gypsy girl.

This surprised Frollo. He wondered if the hunchback could fall in love. Surely not! After all, he cared only about his bells.

By the time Frollo reached the cathedral square, Esmeralda was gone. In her place was a performer dressed in a red and yellow costume. The clownlike figure was balancing a chair between his teeth! Then the priest realized that he knew the performer. It was the poet Gringoire.

"Gringoire! What are you doing?"

The priest's voice made Gringoire lose his balance. The chair tumbled to the ground.

"Claude Frollo! So nice to see you!" replied Gringoire. "This is not as hard as writing poems. Besides, performing gives me more time to spend with Esmeralda."

Frollo's eyes grew dark and frightening.

"Do you know Esmeralda?"

"*Know her?*" Gringoire laughed. "She is my wife, and I am her husband!"

Claude Frollo was stunned. "What are you saying? Is this true?" he demanded.

"Oh, yes," Gringoire said. Then he told the priest the story of his adventure in the Court of Miracles. He told how Esmeralda had saved him from hanging by agreeing to marry him. "But she won't even let me kiss her," he said sadly.

"What do you mean?"

"Well, she won't let me get close to her. There's a charm around her neck. She says it will stop her from loving any man until she finds her mother. When she was a baby, you see, she was separated from her mother. But I think there's another reason."

"Go on!"

Frollo's expression was intense. He seemed to hang on every word Gringoire was saying.

"Well, I think she loves someone else."

"Who?"

"Someone by the name of *Phoebus*. I often hear her whispering his name. And she has taught her little goat to spell it out with blocks: P-H-O-E-B-U-S."

"Phoebus?"

"Yes, the captain of the king's bodyguard. Do you know him, Frollo?"

But there was no answer. The priest had already stormed back inside the cathedral.

* * * *

A few weeks later, Frollo's studies were disturbed by a loud knock on his chamber door. "Enter!" he called out.

It was his brother Jehan. He had come, as he often did, to borrow some money. Frollo was not surprised. "Dear brother," said Jehan. "I am so sorry to bother you. But I need to borrow a little money—for my studies."

Claude Frollo knew his brother well. He knew that Jehan liked to spend time in the taverns, drinking with his friends. "Are you sure you will buy books with it?"

"Yes, of course, dear brother! But if any is left over, I may have a small glass or two with my good friend Phoebus."

"Who?"

"Oh, Captain Phoebus, a gentleman. We're planning to meet tonight at the tavern. But only for a short time. After that, he's meeting with a young lady called Esmeralda."

The priest saw an opportunity. He would give his brother the money to have a drink with Phoebus. Then he would follow him. Perhaps Captain Phoebus would lead him to Esmeralda.

After Jehan left, Frollo reached for his dark cape. He put a small silver dagger in his pocket and blew out the candles. Then he hurried after his brother.

While Jehan and Phoebus were in the tavern, Frollo hid in a nearby doorway. In an hour or so, Jehan and Phoebus came outside and said their farewells.

"Have fun with the girl, Phoebus!" Jehan called out. Then he walked off the other way, tripping on the cobblestones.

Phoebus started walking toward the bridge where he planned to meet Esmeralda. Soon he noticed a dark figure creeping behind him in the shadows.

"Who's there?" he called.

Claude Frollo, his face hidden by his hood, stepped out of the shadows.

"What do you want?" Phoebus asked.

"Just to know if you are seeing the young

gypsy woman tonight. I mean no harm."

"*Why* do you want to know, stranger?"

"I have my reasons. If you are meeting her, prove it. In return, I will give you a bag of gold coins," the hooded man said.

Phoebus thought about it and smiled. "Very well," he said. He could always use a bit of extra money. "Follow me."

They soon reached a house near the St. Michel Bridge. Phoebus turned to Frollo.

"Come inside," he said. "Wait right here until I return. For a bag of gold coins, you can see everything!"

Frollo hid in a dark room. After a short time, he heard Esmeralda and Phoebus come in. He saw the captain undo Esmeralda's cape. Then he saw him put his arms around the lovely young woman and hold her close.

"Oh, Phoebus, I've been dreaming of this moment!" Esmeralda cried in a trembling voice. "Say that you love me—"

Each word tortured Frollo.

"As you wish, my dear. We will talk later," Phoebus told Esmeralda. He began to undo the charm around her neck.

"No, darling! You must leave that alone! I need it to find my mother!" she cried.

Frollo saw that Esmeralda's eyes were flaming like candles in the darkness.

"So you do not love me?" Phoebus asked, his head dizzy from the wine.

"Oh, yes, yes, *yes!*" Esmeralda said. "Of course I love you! I want to marry you!"

She put her arms around his neck. He pulled her closer and kissed her.

Frollo could not bear to watch any longer. He crept out of his hiding place.

"Yes, I do love you, Phoebus, my darling," whispered Esmeralda. She looked up—but instead of seeing the captain, she saw the dark, frightening eyes of another man standing just behind him. He held a gleaming dagger in his hands!

Phoebus felt Esmeralda shudder. He turned to see what had frightened her. Then suddenly, the dagger came slashing down at his chest! Esmeralda screamed. Just as she fell into a faint, she thought she felt a kiss. But what a strange kiss it was! It felt like a hot iron burning her lips.

When the gypsy girl came to her senses, she was surrounded by soldiers on the night watch. The captain had been carried away, bathed in his own blood. The window was wide open, and the priest was gone. What had happened? She heard one soldier saying to another, "This is the witch who stabbed the captain!"

6 Sanctuary!

Outside the Palace of Justice, a few old women were gossiping.

"A gypsy goes on trial today for murdering an officer of the king!"

"Yes—they say she's a witch. I've heard that even her goat can talk with the devil!"

Inside the court, Esmeralda sat alone. She was pale and grief-stricken. All she could think about was Phoebus. "Just tell me if he's still alive," she kept saying.

A witness came to the stand. It was the woman who owned the house where Phoebus had met with Esmeralda. "Two men were there—a handsome captain and another man," the woman said. "He was hidden by a black cloak. Nothing could be seen of him but his eyes, which looked like two burning coals. The handsome captain brought a beautiful young girl back to the room. All of a sudden, I heard a scream from upstairs. Then something hit the floor, and I saw a black form falling past the window to the river below! It looked like a ghost dressed as a priest—but whatever it was started swimming toward the city. When the night watchmen came, we went upstairs. There we found the gypsy, pretending to be dead."

"Bring in the second prisoner," the judge ordered. Esmeralda's goat was led in.

A court official walked up to the goat. He held up Esmeralda's tambourine and asked, "What time is it?"

The goat struck the tambourine seven times. In fact, it was exactly seven o'clock. A shudder of terror swept over the court.

Next, a set of letters was emptied out onto the floor. Djali sorted out the letters to spell the name *Phoebus.*

"The animal is possessed!" declared the judge. He turned to Esmeralda. "You are accused of using sorcery to kill Captain Phoebus. Obviously, this bewitched goat helped you. Do you deny this?"

"Yes, yes! I deny it!" Esmeralda cried out.

The judge sneered. "Then how do you explain the charges being made against you?"

"I cannot explain them, sir. I only know that I am innocent. I love Phoebus! It was a priest—the priest who keeps following me."

The judge became restless. "Very well. I've heard enough of your lies. Off to the torture chamber! You'll soon change your story."

Esmeralda was dragged to a room filled with iron instruments of torture. By a blazing fire, a bearded man prepared red-hot coals with rusty tongs. The roaring furnace provided the only light in the terrible room. In one corner, a clerk sat with pen, ink, and paper—ready to take notes.

The torturers forced the terrified girl to lie down on a leather bed.

"They say you dance," one man said, "so we'll begin with your legs!"

A special boot made of oak and metal was put on one of the gypsy girl's feet. As the boot started to squeeze tighter and tighter, she screamed, "Mercy!"

"Admit that you are guilty!" one of the

torturers demanded harshly. "*Say it!*"

"Yes, yes! I confess. Have mercy!" cried Esmeralda.

"And you are a witch?"

Esmeralda's spirit was broken. "If you say so—yes," she moaned softly.

Led by the guards, Esmeralda hobbled back to the courtroom. Djali's heartbroken bleating echoed her sorrow.

"So, you've confessed!" the judge exclaimed. "Good! Within two months, you will be taken to the Cathedral of Notre Dame. There you will beg for the forgiveness of your soul. At noon of the same day, you will be taken to the city gallows—along with your goat. Both of you shall be hanged by the neck until dead. May God have mercy on your soul."

"Oh, this must be a dream," the horrified girl cried out. Rough hands pulled her away.

Soon she lay in the dungeon, shivering in the darkness, not knowing whether it was day or night. Drops of rainwater fell on the floor from the cracked ceiling. Esmeralda's cell was cold, dark, and damp. She had not a single blanket to keep her warm.

*   *   *   *

Some weeks later, the door of Esmeralda's cell cracked open. A shaft of blinding light entered from the world outside. Then the door closed again. A human form, holding a lantern, stood before her.

"Who are you?" she asked.

"A priest," was the simple answer.

The sound of that familiar voice made her tremble. She knew immediately that her visitor was Claude Frollo.

"Are you ready?" he asked.

"For what?"

"To die. Your execution will be tomorrow."

Esmeralda clenched her pale, thin fingers. "Why have you done this?" she asked sadly. "What have I ever done to harm you? Why should you hate me so?"

"But I *love* you!" Frollo exclaimed.

Her tears suddenly stopped. In spite of her fear, she stared at him in confusion. A drop of cold water fell upon her cheek. She didn't know what to think.

"At one time I was happy in my studies," Frollo said. "Then I saw you wearing that pretty dress as you danced in the square. The sound of your singing entranced me. Since then, I can't get you out of my mind. I have tried to study, but your beauty haunts my thoughts. Yes—I love you! One night, I tried to kidnap you. Do you remember? Please, have pity on me! Return my love now—and I will see that you go free! Save yourself, and end my suffering!"

Esmeralda was stunned. "But I do not love you. I love Phoebus."

"Phoebus is dead! He *must* be dead. Surely my dagger pierced his heart."

"No! Then how can you ask me to go on living?" Esmeralda cried miserably. "Monster! Murderer! Get out of here! Leave me to die! Let my blood stain your soul forever. You ask me to be yours, priest? Never, *never!*"

"Then die!" Frollo yelled. "No one shall have you!" Taking his lantern, he stumbled out, leaving Esmeralda in the darkness.

* * * *

Meanwhile, the recluse Paquette—also known as Sister Gudule—was crying. As usual, she was kissing the pink baby shoe, the only thing of her daughter's that was left to her. She was convinced that the gypsies had killed her baby after stealing it. She looked out the window just as Claude Frollo was crossing the square. As she peered out, she noticed that some men were preparing the gallows. Paquette called out to Frollo as he walked by.

"Father," she asked, "who are they getting ready to hang?"

"A young gypsy girl," the priest said. "The hanging will be tomorrow at noon."

"Good! I *hate* the gypsies! They stole my daughter and ruined my life. And there is one gypsy I hate even more than all the rest. She is very pretty—about the same age that my sweet daughter would have been by now. Every time I see that girl pass by, my blood starts to boil!"

"Well, sister, you can rejoice then," said the priest. "She is the very one who will die tomorrow!"

* * * *

Phoebus, meanwhile, was not dead. Men of his kind are very hard to kill. Not that his wound was slight. In fact, at one point, the doctor thought he might die. But the priest's silver dagger had narrowly missed his heart. As Phoebus slowly healed and grew stronger, he once again began to yearn for the company of women.

Two months after the stabbing, he rode into Paris. He soon found himself at the house of the fair Fleur-de-Lys.

"Phoebus, darling, I've missed you! What have you been doing?" she asked.

"Dreaming of you, my sweet!" he lied.

Fragrant roses were in her hair. As they kissed, Phoebus easily forgot the passion of the gypsy girl.

Then suddenly, Fleur-de-Lys noticed the bandages on Phoebus's chest.

"What happened?" she asked in alarm.

"Oh, I had a quarrel with an officer. We exchanged scratches with our swords. It's nothing to worry about."

To avoid any more questions, Phoebus pointed out the window to the square below. "Do you know why a crowd is gathering out there?" he asked.

"Oh, I heard that they're hanging a gypsy witch and her goat today."

"And what is the name of this witch?"

"I know not," said Fleur-de-Lys.

The captain put his arms around the girl's shoulders. They talked about their wedding, three months ahead. He had not, after all, ever broken their engagement.

On the street below, Esmeralda rattled toward Notre Dame in a small wooden cart. A thick rope already hung around her neck. Djali, her neck also circled with a rope, stood with her. When the doors of Notre Dame opened, the sound of chanting could be heard. It was the Mass for the Dead.

Holding a cross, Frollo stood at the door of the cathedral. He watched as Esmeralda was taken down from the cart.

"My child, are you ready to meet God? Have you begged His forgiveness for your sins?" the archdeacon asked loudly. Then he leaned closer and whispered in her ear. The people watching thought that he was hearing her confession. "Will you be mine?" he whispered. "I can save you even now!"

"Demon! You have no right to say these things to me!"

"But it is not too late! Only tell me that you love me!" Frollo whispered.

"I hate you!"

Mouthing a prayer, Frollo walked away. Esmeralda looked up to the sky for the first time that morning. She was amazed to see Captain Phoebus on a balcony overlooking the square. His arms were around a beautiful young lady.

"Oh, Phoebus! Phoebus!" Esmeralda cried out. She tried to reach out to him, but her arms were tied. "*Phoebus!*"

The young lady who leaned upon Phoebus's chest looked at him angrily. Then she left the balcony and the window closed.

"Phoebus!" Esmeralda called out again. "Do you believe the lies they tell about me?" Then a horrible idea came to her. She fell senseless to the ground.

"Come," said an attendant. "Carry her to the cart. Let's make an end of this business!"

* * * *

High above, from the gallery of the royal

statues, Quasimodo watched the sad scene in the square. No one noticed him there, for his deformed face looked a lot like the ugly stone gargoyles around him.

"Hang the witch!" the crowd shouted.

Quasimodo was ready. He had tied a knotted rope to one of the gallery's small pillars. The end of the rope hung down to the pavement far below. Now he seized the rope with his feet, knees, and hands. In a moment, he was gliding down the front of the cathedral like a drop of rain on a pane of glass! When he reached the ground, he knocked down the executioners with his enormous fists. Then he carried Esmeralda off, as easily as a girl would carry her doll. With one bound he was inside the church, holding the gypsy girl above his head. In a loud voice, the hunchback shouted out, *"Sanctuary! Sanctuary!"*

The crowd was thrilled. The clapping of 10,000 hands caused Quasimodo's only eye to sparkle with joy. *"Sanctuary! Sanctuary!"* the mob repeated.

Esmeralda opened her eyes and looked at Quasimodo. For a moment, she was horror-

stricken at the sight. But she realized that she was safe. Even gypsies knew that churches were places of sanctuary. Escaped prisoners could avoid their punishments as long as they stayed inside.

Quasimodo quickly closed the door and carried Esmeralda to the bell tower. There, he held her up to the sky. The people in the crowd below again greeted him with applause. And again he shouted, in that voice he rarely used and could never hear, *"Sanctuary! Sanctuary! Sanctuary!"*

7 Frollo's Folly

Having already left the cathedral, Claude Frollo knew nothing of what had happened. Wanting to be alone, he had taken a boat across the Seine. There he walked in the hills, lost in his dark thoughts.

"By now, she is dead," he whispered to himself. "I have killed her!"

Frollo felt no sorrow for what he had done. If he had to, he would do it again. He would rather see her in the hands of the hangman than in the arms of the captain. But then he thought of her at the last hour—the cruel rope about her neck! Suddenly, the first waves of guilt swept over him.

The moon was rising when Frollo headed back to Notre Dame. As he opened the great door of the cathedral, he saw a pale glow moving along the gallery above. A white dress!

How could it be? It was *Esmeralda*!

"Oh, God!" thought Frollo. "She has come back from the dead to haunt me!"

Terrified, Frollo hurried to his room. High above, hidden in the dark shadows of the arches, Esmeralda had not seen Frollo.

In the morning, the gypsy was awakened by faint beams of golden sunlight. At first she thought she was in heaven. But then she remembered that Quasimodo had snatched her from the hands of the hangman! Looking down on the checkered rooftops of Paris, she saw that she was in Notre Dame. Then she remembered that Phoebus was still alive—and that he didn't love her anymore.

* * * *

In the Middle Ages, most churches had a cell set aside for a person seeking sanctuary. At Notre Dame it was a small room toward the top of the cathedral. It was here that Quasimodo had placed the gypsy girl.

That morning, Esmeralda was startled to find Quasimodo standing at her door. "Why did you save me?" she asked.

Even though he could not hear her words,

Quasimodo sensed their meaning. "Have you forgotten the day you gave me water when I needed it?" he asked. "You were the only one in the crowd who took pity on me. That water and your look of pity were precious to me— more than I could ever repay. You may have forgotten, but *I* will never forget!"

Then he handed her the white clothing of a young nun. He also brought her some food and drink. But before Esmeralda could thank him, he scurried away.

She looked around the tiny room. It was six feet square, with one small window—not much better than a prison cell! She felt all alone. Would she never have a family or a home? Just then, however, she felt a shaggy head rubbing against her knees. It was her goat, Djali! She had escaped and followed Quasimodo into the crowd! "Oh, my dear little goat!" she said. "I am so glad to see you!"

Quasimodo came back and gave her a small metal whistle. "Take this," he said. "If you ever need me, use it, and I will come." He put the whistle on the floor and left.

As time went by, Esmeralda wondered if

she might someday return to her former life. She thought about Phoebus. In spite of everything, she could not help loving him. Love is like a tree, she thought. It strikes its roots deeply into one's whole being and keeps on growing even if the heart is broken. Sadly, it is never stronger than when it is most unreasonable.

Some details still puzzled her, though. Why hadn't Phoebus come forth to save her? Who was the woman on the balcony? Perhaps it was his sister. After all, Phoebus told Esmeralda that he loved only her. Perhaps, she thought, Phoebus himself had become confused. After all, Esmeralda had confessed to the crimes. If only she'd been able to withstand the torture, Phoebus would have no reason to doubt her.

Then one day Esmeralda saw Phoebus walking in the square below.

Quasimodo watched her, his heart breaking. "Shall I go and get him?" he asked. He loved Esmeralda—but it was clear that she loved only Phoebus.

Esmeralda uttered a great cry of joy.

Quasimodo hurried down the staircase, holding in his own tears. By the time he reached the square, however, Phoebus had gone into Fleur-de-Lys's house. It was after midnight when the captain came back out, but Quasimodo was still waiting.

The hunchback reached out and stopped him.

"What is your business, vile creature?" Phoebus snarled.

"A lady who loves you waits for you!" Quasimodo replied respectfully.

"Must I go to all the women who say they love me? Tell your lady that I am going to be married!" Phoebus snapped.

"But it is the young gypsy girl. I believe that you know Esmeralda," Quasimodo said.

Phoebus was amazed to hear that she was still alive! In fact, he thought that she had been dead for a month! Phoebus's horse snorted at the ugly bell-ringer.

"The gypsy?" Phoebus exclaimed. He couldn't believe what he was hearing. "What, then—are you from the other world?"

Suddenly, Phoebus was terrified. Striking

Quasimodo with his whip, he rode off.

When she saw Quasimodo returning without Phoebus, Esmeralda's heart sank. That night, she cried herself to sleep.

Meanwhile, the archdeacon heard the story of Esmeralda's rescue. "So," he thought, "that was *not* her ghost I saw! She is alive!" Images of Esmeralda began to haunt him. He yearned to spend all his waking hours near her—just as Quasimodo was doing!

For several days, Frollo refused to come out of his room. From his window he could see Esmeralda, sometimes with Djali, and sometimes with Quasimodo. He saw how the hunchback doted on her. This made him more and more jealous.

One evening Frollo could bear it no longer. He *had* to see her! He opened a small drawer and took out a key. Lighting a lantern, he silently tiptoed toward her cell.

Esmeralda was a very light sleeper. She woke as soon as the key turned in the lock. Then, just before Frollo blew out the lantern, Esmeralda saw his face. "Oh, no!" she cried out faintly. "It's the priest!"

"Have pity on me!" Frollo cried out. "My love for you is like a terrible fire. It's like a thousand daggers in my heart! *Love me!*" He held her tightly as she struggled to get away.

"Help! Help!" she cried, as she tried to fight off the priest. But he was too strong for her. With her last bit of strength, she reached out for Quasimodo's whistle and blew it as hard as she could.

Seconds later, Frollo felt a powerful arm pulling him away from Esmeralda. In the darkness, Frollo could not clearly see who it was—but he thought it must be Quasimodo. Then he saw a gleaming sword being raised over his head. "Quasimodo!" he yelled, forgetting that the bell-ringer was deaf. Frollo was sure that he was about to die!

Then, suddenly, Quasimodo hesitated. "No! No blood upon her!" he cried out. Frollo felt himself being pulled away.

As the moon shone on Frollo's face, Quasimodo saw who it was. He dropped to his knees in surprise. "My lord," he said, solemnly offering Frollo the sword. "Kill me first, and do what you please afterward."

But Esmeralda was standing right behind him. She snatched the sword and held it high. "You won't come close now, coward priest!" she cried out fiercely.

Frollo said nothing. He kicked Quasimodo aside and disappeared into the cathedral.

As Esmeralda fell on her bed sobbing, the priest groped his way back to his cell. His thoughts whirled, insane with jealousy.

"Nobody shall have her!" he muttered to himself. "*Nobody!*"

8 Gringoire's Idea

The archdeacon had an evil plan. A few days later, he tracked down Pierre Gringoire. "I have some news about your wife," he told the poet. "Parliament has discussed her case and made an exception to the rules. Within three days she will be taken from her sanctuary and hanged. You must save her!"

"But *how*, Frollo?" Gringoire asked.

"Go to her. She trusts you. Change clothes with her and allow her to escape. Of course— when you're found out—you will probably have to hang in her place. But at least you will have saved her."

"But, Frollo, I don't *want* to die!"

"Gringoire! Don't you remember how she once saved you? You are in her debt!"

The poet thought for a moment. Then he came up with an idea. "Frollo," he said.

"There is another way. King Clopin and the outcasts of the Court of Miracles must help. But they all like Esmeralda—I know they will want to save her."

Frollo was happy. All he wanted was to get Esmeralda out of Notre Dame and away from Quasimodo. It didn't really matter how.

That very night, the vagabonds, thieves, and gypsies of the Court of Miracles gathered together. They had all kinds of weapons—axes, swords, crossbows, and daggers. In the darkness, they made their way across Paris, to the square in front of Notre Dame.

"Bring out the gypsy!" Clopin yelled out. "Give her to us or we'll attack!"

Quasimodo was horrified. He thought they had come to hang Esmeralda. He didn't know they wanted to save her. So he threw big rocks down on the crowd.

"Break down the door! Smash it! Let's get inside!" Clopin shouted.

Quasimodo did all he could to stop them. He threw more rocks down on their heads. Then he remembered that the cathedral's roof had been repaired that day. He soon found some leftover wooden beams and coils of lead. With superhuman strength, he lifted up a heavy beam and threw it over the side of the cathedral. When it landed on the square below, the cries of the dying filled the night.

"What are you waiting for, men?" Clopin shrieked. "Use that beam as a battering ram!"

Quasimodo could hear the front doors breaking. He was losing the battle! But then he remembered the lead coils. After lighting a fire with his lantern, he heaped the coils on top. Then he poured the molten lead along the gutter and watched. Soon bright, hot streams ran out of the gargoyles' mouths! Screams filled the air as the hot lead poured down on the outcasts below.

Now Quasimodo was winning. Frollo ran up to Gringoire, who was watching from a distance. "Gringoire, your plan won't work! It seems that Quasimodo would gladly die in order to save her. We must get to her *now!*"

"But, Frollo, how will we get in?"

"I have the keys to the towers! Hurry!"

"But how will we get out?"

"We'll leave by the back way. I have all the

keys we need. I also have a boat ready. We can row to the other side of the Seine!"

Gringoire and Frollo hurried into the cathedral. As they entered Esmeralda's cell, Frollo stayed hidden in the shadows so she couldn't see his face. Gringoire did all the talking, so she wouldn't hear Frollo's voice. Before long, the two men led Esmeralda and Djali down the stairs and out the back way to the waiting boat. They could still hear the noise and confusion in the square.

By now, the king's soldiers had arrived. Led by Captain Phoebus, they were fighting the outcasts, cutting them down like flies. When Quasimodo saw what was happening, he fell on his knees and lifted his hands to heaven. He joyfully ran to Esmeralda's cell, eager to tell her that she had been saved once again. When he found her cell empty, his heart sank.

9   The Little Shoe

Frollo rowed the boat across the river as fast as he could. Esmeralda watched his movements suspiciously. The man's hood was pulled down to mask his face. But something about him looked familiar.

The noise around Notre Dame was getting louder. Everyone in the boat could hear the crowd shouting, "The gypsy! The witch! Death to the gypsy girl!" Esmeralda was in despair. Alas, it seemed that Quasimodo had been wrong. She had not been saved after all. Now a mob wanted to hang her. Esmeralda hid her face in her hands.

Meanwhile, Gringoire was deep in thought. Somehow he felt closer to Djali than to Esmeralda. After all, Esmeralda would have nothing to do with him—while Djali was always friendly! He knew that Djali had been sentenced to hang along with Esmeralda. Looking first at the gypsy and then at the goat, he muttered to himself, "I cannot save you both."

When the little boat reached the shore, Gringoire ran off with Djali before Frollo could stop him. This left Esmeralda alone with the man in the black cloak. Suddenly she felt the stranger's hand in hers. It was strong and cold. He led her along the river and over a bridge. Finally, they reached the square where the hangings took place. The man stopped, turned to her, and lifted his hood.

"No!" she cried. "I *knew* it!"

"Listen to me," the priest said. "This is serious. There's been a special meeting of Parliament. They've decided to turn you over to the hangman again. I tried to save you, but they're still after you. Can't you see that I'm not lying to you? *I love you.* There's still time to save yourself. I've arranged everything for you to get away. Your fate is up to you. Now you must take your choice." He let go of her hand and pointed to himself. With his other hand, he pointed to the gallows. "Choose between the two of us now," he said coldly.

Frollo waited for her answer. At last the miserable girl cried out, "The noose is less horrible to me than you are!"

"You have no idea how much I love you," Frollo insisted. "I don't want to see you die. You don't have to say you love me. Just say that you *want* to love me. That would be enough. One word of kindness is all I ask!"

"You are a murderer!" Esmeralda cried out. "I love Phoebus. Leave me alone!"

"Die, then!" Frollo snarled. He dragged her toward the tiny house where the recluse lived. "Sister Gudule!" he cried. "Here's the gypsy girl. Take your revenge!"

A bony arm came through a barred window and held Esmeralda's arm tightly.

"Hold her," the priest ordered. "Don't let her go for any reason. I'll go get the soldiers. Then you shall see her hanged."

A low laugh came from inside the house.

The priest left, hurrying down the street toward Notre Dame.

The girl looked through the bars at the recluse. Panting with terror, she tried to pull away. But Paquette held her with incredible strength. Now the fear of death came over Esmeralda. Her thoughts were of life, of her childhood, of the beauty of nature, of love, of Phoebus. Then she remembered what was coming. She could hear the eerie laugh of the recluse. "Ha, ha! You are going to be hanged!" the cruel voice taunted.

Esmeralda peered through the bars at the woman's face. "What have I done to you? Why do you hate me so?"

"What have you done to me?" Paquette asked. "Well, listen! I had a child, you see, a pretty little girl. Your people stole my baby— and my heart! That's what you did to me."

"Maybe I wasn't even born then," the young girl pleaded.

"Oh, yes," Paquette said. "She would have been about your age now. For 15 years, I have been suffering. The gypsy women stole my baby and then killed her. All I have left is one little shoe. Here, let me show you. Look! This is the only thing I have to remember her."

With that, the recluse showed the gypsy girl the tiny pink shoe.

"My God! Oh, my God!" Esmeralda cried. With her free hand, she tore open the little bag she wore about her neck. Reaching inside, she took out a tiny shoe just like the other. A piece of paper was attached to the shoe with these words on it:

> *When you find its match,*
> *Your mother will stretch*
> *out her arms to you!*

Paquette compared the two shoes, read the paper, and then stared at Esmeralda. "My daughter! You are my *daughter!*"

"My mother!" the gypsy girl cried.

The wall and the iron bars separated them. Paquette dropped Esmeralda's arm, ran to the door, and pulled her daughter inside.

She kissed Esmeralda and held her tightly. "My child, my daughter! I have my daughter again! Here she is! We will leave this place. I have money in our own country. We shall go there to live. We shall have fields and a house. You shall sleep in a big bed! Oh, merciful God! Who would believe I have my daughter again? We shall be so happy!"

Just then, they heard horses approaching. The gypsy girl threw herself into her mother's arms. "Save me, save me, Mother! They are coming for me!"

Paquette turned pale. "Who's coming for you? And why? What have you done?"

"I don't know," answered the poor girl. "But I've been sentenced to death!"

"To *death!*" exclaimed her mother.

"Yes, my mother. They want to kill me. They're coming to hang me."

"Hide in that dark corner over there," Paquette said. "They won't see you there. I'll tell them you fought me off and escaped."

Soon a voice rang out. "This way, Captain Phoebus," Frollo shouted. At the sound of that name, Esmeralda whimpered and stirred.

"Don't move, child!" Paquette whispered. "Be quiet!"

By now, a crowd of men and horses were gathered around the tiny house. They called out for the gypsy girl. Paquette cracked the door to talk to them. "She bit my arm and ran away," she said.

Both mother and daughter held their breath as the men talked outside. "Come on," said one. "She wouldn't be here. This old woman hates gypsies—especially the little dancing girl with the goat."

Some of the other men agreed with him.

"Let's go on, then," their leader finally said. "We must keep searching. The king has ordered it." Just before the men rode away, Esmeralda heard another man speaking.

"Sir, it is not my job to hang witches. I leave you to do your own dirty work. I must go back to my men, who are waiting for their captain."

It was Captain Phoebus!

Before her mother could stop her, Esmeralda rushed to the window. "Phoebus!" she cried out. "Here, my Phoebus!"

But Phoebus had already galloped around the corner. The other men were still there, however. They jumped off their horses and ran into Paquette's house.

"Oh, Mother, help me!" Esmeralda cried.

"My child!" shrieked Paquette. She clung to Esmeralda as the soldiers dragged them both away. "But she is my daughter!" cried Paquette. "See—here is her little pink shoe! She's my *daughter!* You can't take her!"

Mother and daughter were being pulled toward the ladder that led to the gallows. Paquette was frantic. She sank her teeth into the hangman's hand. As the executioner howled in pain, a soldier pushed Paquette away. Her head slammed down on the ground. She was dead.

The hangman laughed. Then, carrying the young girl over his shoulder, he climbed up the ladder. "The king wills it," he said.

§10 Quasimodo's Sorrow

Quasimodo was desperate when he saw that Esmeralda's cell was empty. He ran through the church looking for her. He tried to guess who could have taken her. Then he remembered that Claude Frollo was the only one with a key to her cell. The scene with Frollo and the whistle also came back to him. Now he had no doubt that Frollo had taken Esmeralda. Yet he loved Frollo, and even now he tried not to be angry with him.

As dawn broke, Quasimodo saw Frollo returning to Notre Dame. He watched his old friend climb up the tower staircase. He had no idea what he would do if he actually confronted the priest.

At the very top of the tower, Quasimodo watched as the priest looked down on the town. He stole up behind him, wanting to ask what he had done with the gypsy girl. But the priest was staring hard at something, so Quasimodo followed his gaze.

A ladder stood against the gallows. A girl dressed in white was being carried up the ladder. There was a noose around her neck. Quasimodo gasped. It was Esmeralda!

Once he reached the platform of the gallows, the man arranged the noose. Then he kicked away the ladder. Quasimodo could scarcely breathe. The girl was swinging from the end of the rope!

The priest gave a terrible laugh—such as can come only from one who is not truly human. Quasimodo didn't hear the laugh, but he saw it and understood. Without thinking, he rushed at the priest in fury and pushed Claude Frollo over the edge.

Frollo landed on a narrow ledge before sliding down to a gutter. There he clung to a gargoyle and struggled to get a foothold. Quasimodo had only to stretch out his hand to pull Frollo back—but he didn't even look at the priest. Instead, he was staring at the gypsy girl. His heart was crushed. A steady

stream of tears flowed over his deformed face.

At last, Frollo lost his grip. Quasimodo watched as he fell screaming to his death 200 feet below. Then he raised his eyes to look upon the gypsy girl. He could see her body, hanging from the gallows. It was twitching in the last struggles of death. Then, in utter despair, he looked down at the archdeacon. With a sob that shook deep in his chest, he cried out, "*Oh, all that I ever loved!*"

Quasimodo disappeared from Notre Dame that very evening. The poor hunchback was never seen again—nor was it ever known what became of him.

At sunset, the hangman's helpers took Esmeralda's body down. As was the custom, they put it in the cellar at Montfaucon. In this wretched place, criminals, outcasts, and the poor were buried in a common grave.

* * * *

Two years later, three men went to Montfaucon to dig up the corpse of Louis XI's barber. The new king had recently granted the barber a pardon. His family was now allowed to bury him in his own grave in their parish church cemetery.

As the workers searched among all the bodies, two skeletons were found locked together. One was that of a woman. The bones of her hand clutched a little pouch, which was open and empty. The other skeleton was that of a man. His backbone was horribly twisted and one leg was a good bit shorter than the other. But the man's neck was not broken.

The workers were astounded. It was clear that this man had not been hanged. He had come to Montfaucon on his own and died there! When the workers tried to separate this skeleton from the one that it embraced, it crumbled to dust.